This book belongs to:

. . . .

. . . .

Editor: Lucy Cuthew
Designer: Cathy Tincknell
Series Editor: Ruth Symons
Editorial Director: Victoria Garrard
Art Director: Laura Roberts-Jensen

Copyright © QEB Publishing, Inc. 2014

First published in the United States by QEB Publishing, Inc.
3 Wrigley, Suite A, Irvine, CA 92618

www.qed-publishing.co.uk

A CIP record for this book is available from the Library of Congress.

ISBN 978 1 60992 700 4

Printed in China

Give Us a Smile, Cinderella

Written by Steve Smallman

Illustrated by Marcin Piwowarski

QEB Publishing

Once upon a time there was a young girl called Cinderella. She lived in a big house with her mean old stepmother and two horrible stepsisters, Griselda and Prunella.

They made poor Cinderella do all of the housework while they lazed about eating sweets.

Griselda and Prunella were so lazy that they couldn't even be bothered to brush their teeth!

Their teeth went yellow,   then green,

then brown,   and some of them even fell out.

The stepsisters often had toothaches too, which made them even meaner.

Poor Cinderella worked hard all day. But no matter how tired she was, she always brushed her teeth twice a day —once in the morning and again just before bedtime.

When she went to sleep, Cinderella dreamed that she was married to a handsome prince, lived in a beautiful castle, and never had to do any housework. Ever!

As it happened, there was a handsome prince called Rupert in a castle not very far away. His dad (the King) wanted Rupert to get married and he had a genius idea!

"We'll hold a ball!"
he cried excitedly.

"What, a soccer ball?"
asked Rupert.

"No! Not a *soccer* ball," said the king. "A *ball* ball! A big fancy party.

You're bound to find the girl of your dreams, and we'll have the wedding the week after!"

So that was settled.

A few days later the invitations to the royal ball were sent out.

"Look! There's one for me!" gasped Cinderella.

"Yes, but you can't go!" sneered Griselda.

"That's right," said Prunella, "you have nothing to wear."

The stepsisters made Cinderella brush their hair.

Then they made her lace them into their ball gowns.

Finally, the stepsisters and their mother went to the ball, leaving Cinderella at home on her own.

Cinderella sat
on the floor and
started to cry.
Then . . .

POOOOF!

a beautiful lady
appeared in a
cloud of smoke!

"Who are you?" gasped Cinderella.

"I am your fairy godmother!"
said the lady. "Cinderella,
you *shall* go to the ball!"

POOF!

"Here's your ball gown!"

POOF!

"Here are your glass slippers, and . . ."

POOF!

"here are your coach and horses!"

"Magic!"
gasped Cinderella.

"Well, yes!" chuckled
her fairy godmother.
"But the magic will
only last until
midnight, so make
sure you're home
by then!"

"Oh Dad, I'll never find the girl of my dreams,"
Prince Rupert moaned to the King.

"I've just danced with two girls
with terrible teeth and
breath like stinky cheese!"

"Keep trying, my boy,"
said the King.

Just then, a girl walked in with the most
beautiful smile Rupert had ever seen!

"Who's that?" said
Griselda and Prunella.

They had no idea it was Cinderella!

Prince Rupert was in love!
He wouldn't dance with anyone
else for the rest of the night.

At the end of the
evening he took
Cinderella's hand
and said, "Will
you be my . . ."

BONG, BONG, BONG . . .

The clock started to strike midnight!

BONG, BONG, BONG . . .

Cinderella ran through the crowded ballroom.

BONG, BONG, BONG . . .

One of her shoes fell off.

BONG, BONG, BONG!

Cinderella had just skidded through the palace doors when . . .

POOF!

she was back in her raggedy
old dress again.

"Oh, drats!" cried Prince Rupert.
"The girl of my dreams has
disappeared!"

Then he saw Cinderella's tiny
glass slipper and had a great idea!

He would ask every girl in the
kingdom to try on the shoe, and
whoever it fit, he would marry!

So the Prince trailed around the kingdom looking for his true love, but the shoe didn't fit anyone!

At last he arrived at Cinderella's house. Griselda, Prunella, and Cinderella all tried on the shoe.

And, oh dear, it fitted all of them!
Then the Prince said,

"I know, smile
for me!"

So Prunella smiled.

Griselda smiled.

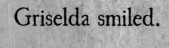

And Cinderella smiled, too.

"It's really you!"
said the Prince.
"Your smile
is magical."

"There's no magic involved,"
said Cinderella, "just toothpaste!"

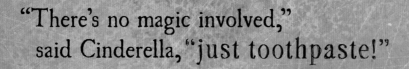

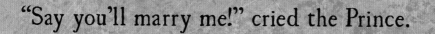

"Say you'll marry me!" cried the Prince.

"Well . . . let me see *your* smile first,"
said Cinderella.

The prince smiled, showing
a row of sparkly white teeth.

"Okay, then!"
said Cinderella.

And they lived
happily ever after!

Next steps

Show the children the cover again. When they first saw it, did they think that they already knew this story? How is this story different from the traditional story? Which parts are the same?

Cinderella's stepmother and stepsisters ate lots of sweets. Ask the children if they know what happens to your teeth if you do that. What happened to Prunella and Griselda's teeth?

Prince Rupert thought that Prunella and Griselda's breath smelled awful! Why do the children think it was so bad? Do the children brush their teeth? How often do they do it? Ask them why they think it's important.

Prince Rupert thought that Cinderella's smile was "magical." Was it magic that gave her such a lovely smile? If not, what was it? Ask the children what happens when you smile at someone.

When Cinderella went to sleep at night she dreamed that she was married to a handsome prince and lived in a beautiful castle. Ask the children what they dream about.

Ask the children if they would like a fairy godmother. What would they wish for if they had one? Ask the children to draw a picture of their fairy godmother.